Arlene Sardine

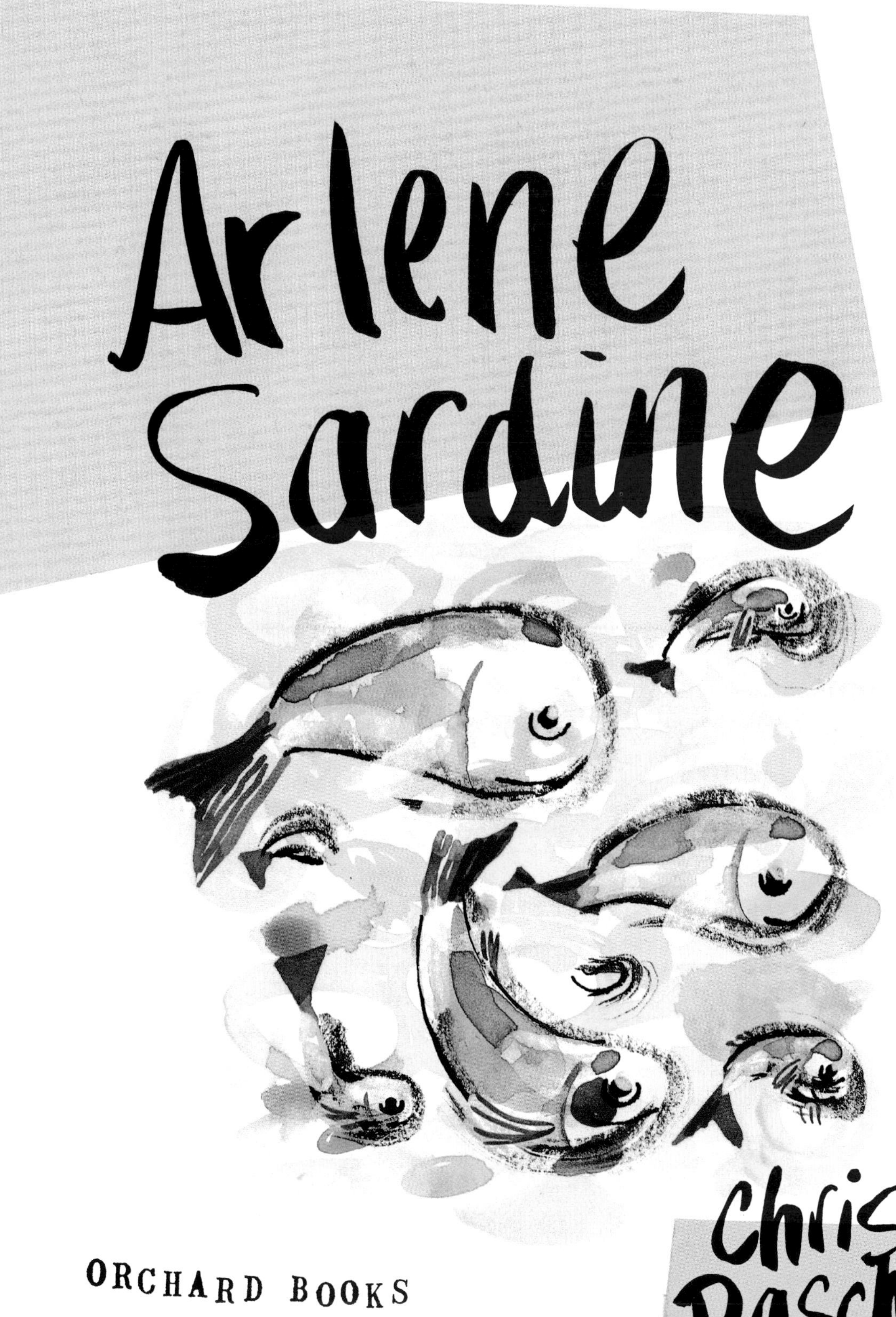

Chris Raschka

ORCHARD BOOKS
NEW YORK

Orchard Books, 95 Madison Avenue, New York, NY 10016

Manufactured in the United States of America
Printed by Barton Press, Inc. Bound by Horowitz/Rae. Book design by Chris Raschka
The text of this book is hand-lettered. The illustrations are watercolor.

10 9 8 7 6 5 4 3 2 1

Library of Congress Cataloging-in-Publication Data
Raschka, Chris.
Arlene sardine / by Chris Raschka. p. cm.
Summary: Follows the short life of Arlene, from brisling to canned sardine.
ISBN 0-531-30111-7 (trade alk. paper). — ISBN 0-531-33111-3 (lib. bdg. : alk. paper)
[1. Sardines—Fiction.] I. Title.
PZ7.R181475 Ar 1998 [E]—dc21 98-12018

for my grandparents

So you want to
be a sardine.

I knew a little fish once who wanted to be a sardine.

Her name was Arlene.

Arlene wanted to be a sardine.

Arlene was born
in a fjord.

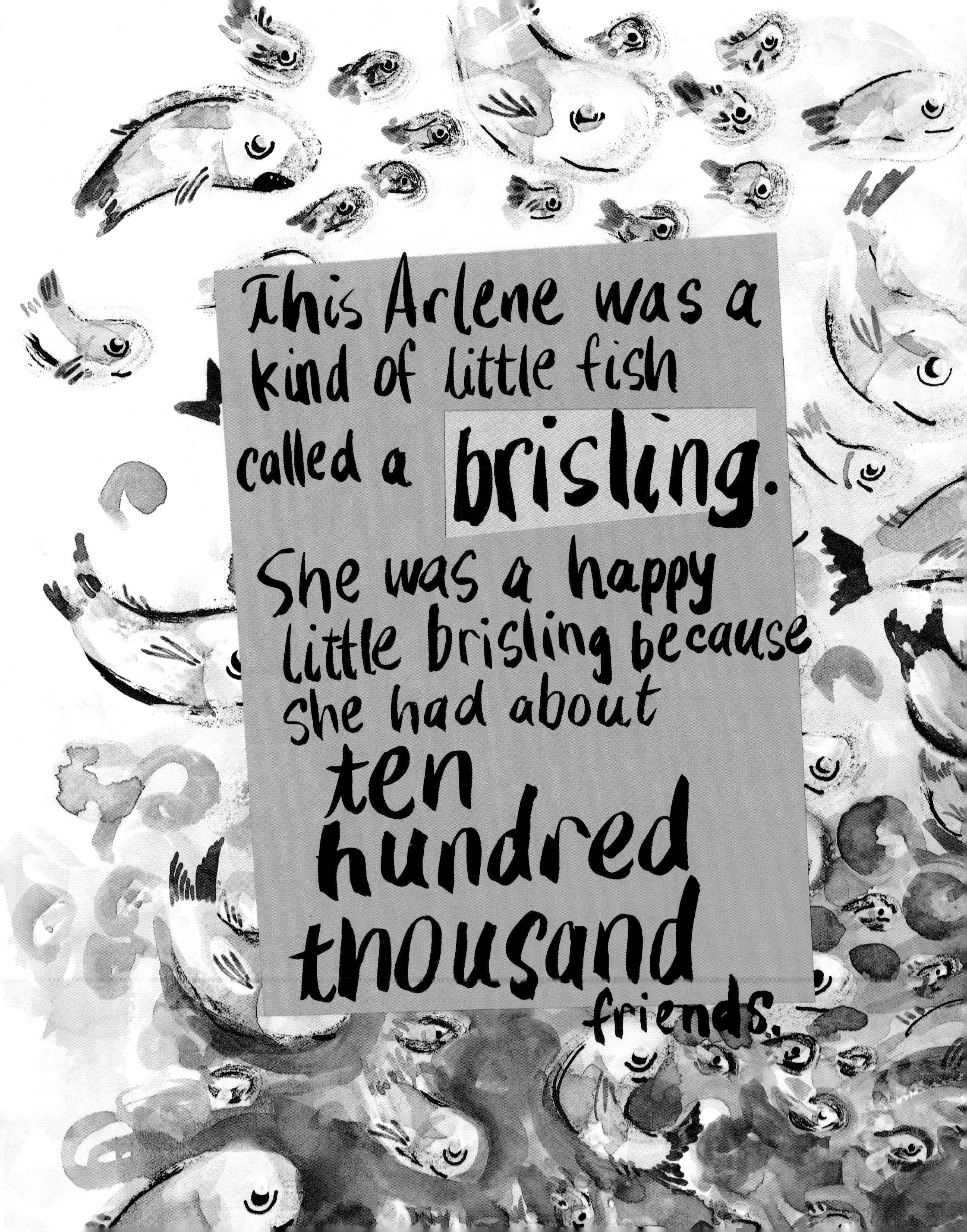
This Arlene was a
kind of little fish
called a brisling.
She was a happy
little brisling because
she had about
ten
hundred
thousand
friends.

ARLENE

First they swam
this way.

Then they swam **that** way.

When Arlene was two, she was fully grown. For a little fish, she was grown-up, grown up enough to become a sardine.

First thing
Arlene swam into
a big net,
a purse net,
a big purse
net.

Arlene swam around in the net for three days and three nights and did not eat anything, so her stomach would be empty. There is a word for this. The word is thronging.

On the third day, the net was lifted out of the water and emptied onto the deck of a fishing boat.

Here, on the deck
of the fishing boat,
Arlene died.

However, Arlene's story is not over, because she was put on ice, in a box, with her friends.

Arlene sailed to the factory.

Machines there,
grading machines,
sorted Arlene in between
other fish her size.

Arlene took a **short, salty bath.**

Then she was

smoked, delicately.

She was

delicately smoked.

Delicately smoked

was she.

I'll bet Arlene felt well rested on the

conveyer belt.

When Arlene reached the big packing room, she was picked up

and put into a little can, a 1/4 dingley can.

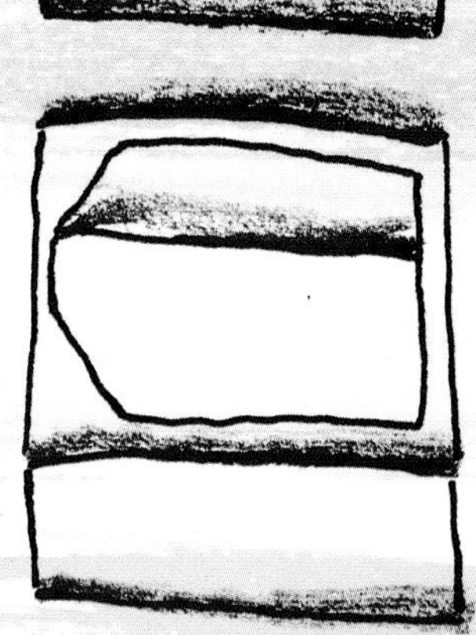

which could be like this:

(2 LAYERS)

or like this:

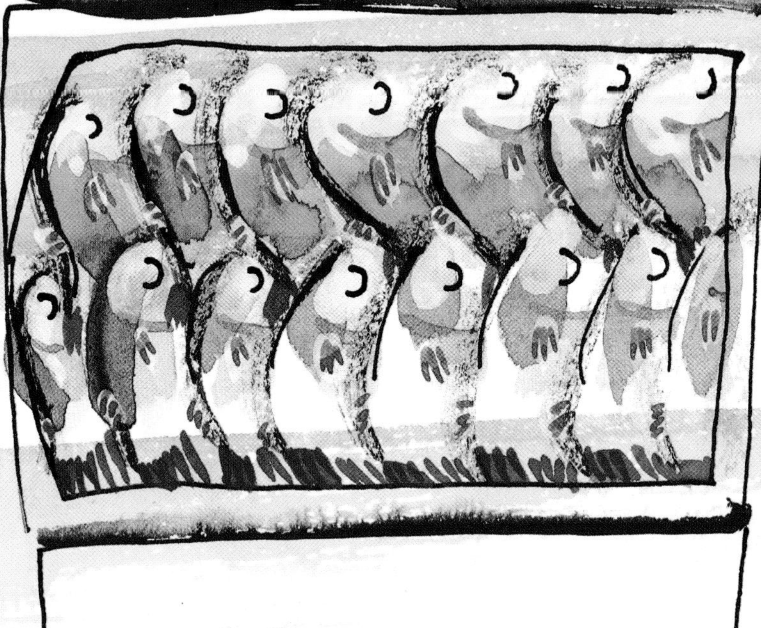

(CROSSPACKED)

or like this:

(1 LAYER)

I wonder if Arlene was a little nervous for the final inspection.

Last thing
Arlene was covered in oil,
olive oil, closed up
with no air inside,
hermetically,
and cooked in her can.

At last, Arlene was a little fish, in oil, packed in a can.

A little fish packed in oil, in a can, is a

Sardine.

Arlene was a Sardine.

SARDINES

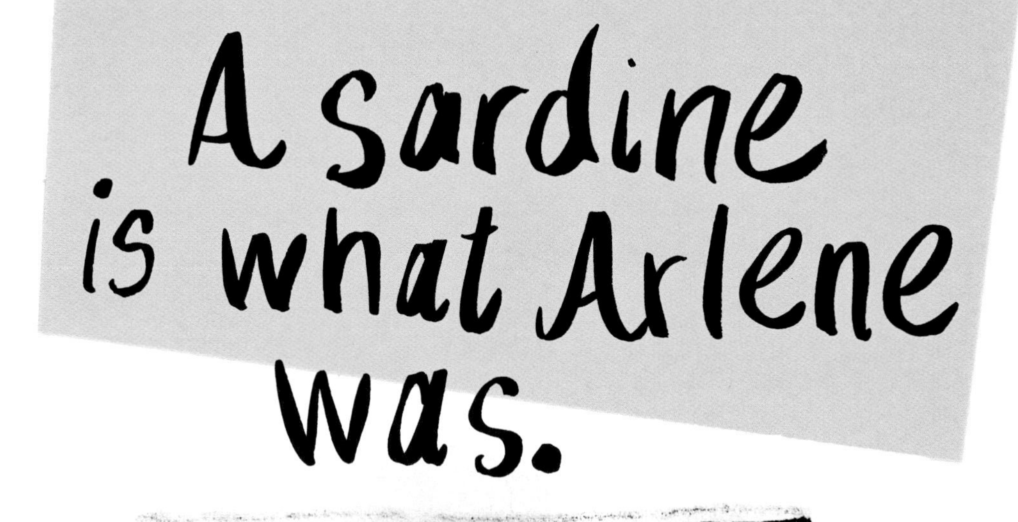
A sardine
is what Arlene
was.